THE GOLDEN
GLOVE

FRED BOWEN

PEACHTREE
ATLANTA

Ω

Published by
PEACHTREE PUBLISHERS
1700 Chattahoochee Avenue
Atlanta, Georgia 30318-2112

www.peachtree-online.com

Cover design by Thomas Gonzalez and Maureen Withee
Book design by Melanie McMahon Ives and Loraine M. Joyner

Printed in the United States of America
10 9 8 7 6 5 4 3 2 1
First Revised Edition

Library of Congress Cataloging-in-Publication Data

Bowen, Fred.
The golden glove / written by Fred Bowen. -- 1st rev. ed.
p. cm.
Summary: When Jamie, a twelve-year-old shortstop, loses the glove that "magically" helped him make fantastic catches, he wonders whether it was the sole secret of his success. Includes a history of baseball gloves.
ISBN 978-1-56145-505-8 / 1-56145-505-9
[1. Baseball--Fiction. 2. Lost and found possessions--Fiction. 3. Self-confidence--Fiction. 4. Fathers and sons--Fiction.] I. Title.
PZ7.B6724Go 2009
[Fic]--dc22
2009016857

To the memory of my father and Little League coach, Thomas J. Bowen.

One

One fine, breezy Saturday morning, the first good Saturday morning after a long, cold winter, the telephone rang in Jamie Bennett's house.

"Hello," Jamie said, with a bit of sleep still in his voice.

"Hey, Jamie," shouted Alex Hammond, Jamie's best friend. "Everybody's getting together to play baseball today."

"Where?" Jamie asked, suddenly wide awake.

"Green Street. On the big field."

"When?"

"In about half an hour."

"Great. I'll be there."

"Don't forget your glove," Alex reminded him.

"Don't worry, I won't."

After a quick breakfast, Jamie put on his baseball shirt—an orange T-shirt with "GIANTS" printed in block letters across the front and the number "8" on the back—and ran to his closet. He reached up on tiptoes and pulled down his glove from the cluttered closet shelf.

The glove looked great—even tied shut with old shoelaces. Jamie sat at the edge of his bed and happily loosened the shoelaces one by one. When he was finished, the glove yawned open and Jamie removed the baseball he had placed there so carefully last winter.

He had taken good care of his glove just as he had been instructed to do.

"Put a few drops of oil in the pocket," Pete had said. Pete Bikakis was the owner of the sports shop in town. "Then take a smooth, dry rag and rub the oil around the pocket. Let the glove sit for a while so the oil will dry. Then toss a ball around with it for a while. Wrap it up with the ball still inside and put it in a nice, safe place. Take it out and oil it a couple more times during the winter. Treat it right and it will treat you right in the spring."

Jamie had followed all of Pete's instructions. Now, the tan leather around the middle of the glove was darkened from the neat's-foot oil he had smoothed on the glove throughout the long winter months.

Although the leather was a rich, dark brown, Jamie could still make out the signature in the center: José Reyes, a shortstop. Just like Jamie.

Jamie slipped his left hand into the cool leather and smiled. The glove felt just as wonderful as the first day he had tried it on at Pete's Sports Shop a year ago.

Jamie and a couple of his friends had stopped by Pete's after school and had tried on a few gloves just for fun. Jamie was not really looking for a new glove, but when his fingers slid into the José Reyes model, he knew he had to have it.

That night, Jamie begged his parents to buy him the glove.

"I don't know, Jamie," his father said cautiously. "That's a lot of money for a baseball glove."

"Please, Dad. It could be an early birthday present."

"You already have a glove."

"I know, Dad, but this one is perfect," Jamie pleaded. "If I had this glove, I could be the best fielder in town."

Jamie's parents looked at each other.

"Okay," his father said, "but you'd better take good care of it."

"I promise!" said Jamie.

Now, a year later, Jamie looked at the glove and how perfectly it had molded to his hand. The glove had been a good-luck charm throughout last year's season. His fielding had improved, and his team had won most of its games.

He took the ball from the well-formed pocket and flipped it high into the air over and over again. He started imagining himself as a real-life major leaguer catching the ball with smooth backhand grabs, basket catches, and over-the-shoulder stabs.

"Bennett's going way back," Jamie said in his best baseball-announcer voice as he lofted the ball across his bedroom.

"He leaps." Jamie dove toward his bed with his glove stretched out to the falling ball.

"He's got it. What a catch by Bennett!" Jamie announced, sprawled on the covers and clutching the ball happily.

The glove was still perfect.

Then with a smile and a whoop of pure joy, Jamie headed out the door to another season of baseball.

Two

Jamie lived in a house on a small hill above Green Street Park. It was the perfect place for a twelve-year-old boy who was crazy about sports.

But on this morning, Jamie barely noticed the park's tennis courts, football field, or basketball courts. His eyes went straight to the baseball diamond. He saw that a group of the neighborhood kids had already started to gather there, so he sprinted down the hill to join them.

As Jamie hopped the center-field fence, Alex turned and waved Jamie over. "Here comes our shortstop," he called. "Come on, we're picking teams."

Jamie exchanged high fives with Alex and joined the circle.

Jamie recognized most of the kids from the town's junior baseball league. Two brothers, Danny and Billy Porter, stood in the middle barking orders and insisting that they play on the same team.

"Billy and I gotta be on one team or we don't play," said Danny.

"No way, that's not fair," Alex shouted. "You guys will kill us."

"Tough. Billy and I play together."

"Who died and made you guys king?" Alex asked.

"We'll give you first pick," said Billy.

Alex shook his head and glanced at Jamie.

"How about we get the first *two* picks?" Jamie suggested.

"All right, but then we get first ups," Billy snapped.

"Okay," Alex said, scanning the group. "I got Jamie and Nick."

"Adam," Danny said quickly.

"Chris."

"Taylor."

"Colin."

"Karen."

As the names were called, players moved toward one of the two team captains. The captains kept calling names until the last player was chosen.

Billy reminded them, "We got first ups."

Jamie trotted out to shortstop and punched his glove. He was ready to play.

The first batter, Danny Porter, stepped to the plate.

"No batter, no batter," Jamie chattered.

Danny cracked a hot smash to Jamie's right. Jamie took a couple of quick steps, reached his glove across his body and made a backhand catch. He planted his right foot in the dirt and threw to first. Danny was out by a step.

Jamie's teammates roared their approval.

"What a play."

"Call ESPN! That's a glove gem."

Danny Porter stared in disbelief and then threw his hat against the dugout fence.

Billy Porter stepped to the plate next. He

lashed a hard grounder to Jamie's left. Jamie glided over toward second base, scooped up the spinning ball, and blazed a perfect throw to first. The field was filled with cheers again.

"That's two!"

"Next batter!"

Adam Larson lofted a soft liner over second. Jamie was off at the crack of the bat. Running toward center field, Jamie glanced back over his shoulder. With his last step, he leaped with his glove stretched out to the falling ball. He tumbled onto the soft outfield grass and held the ball aloft in triumph.

"What a catch by Bennett!" Alex shouted as the team streamed in from the field.

"One-two-three inning."

"Move over José Reyes, make way for Jamie!"

Jamie laughed and looked at his glove. It was perfect.

The game went on for hours with no one keeping score. Kids came and went, switching positions, switching teams, just playing in the Saturday sun.

Jamie played mostly shortstop, making play after play. Some were routine, but some were spectacular.

The glove was like magic. Every ball seemed to find a way into its pocket as if drawn by some invisible force. Armed with that glove, Jamie could do no wrong.

At the end of a long day of baseball, Jamie and Alex ambled over to the soda machine. Alex plunked in some quarters, punched one of the buttons, and grabbed the soda as it came shooting out. Then the two boys sat down against the backside of the outfield fence and Alex took a sip of the soda. A friendly black Labrador retriever raced up to the boys and nuzzled his wet nose against their faces. Alex pushed the dog away.

The dog belonged to Greta "Gretzky" Pemberton. On Saturdays Greta was usually on the basketball court. Alex looked over in the direction of the courts and spotted Greta going for a layup.

"Greta, get your dog out of here, will ya?" yelled Alex. "We're trying to drink our soda and dog spit kills the taste."

"Mingo!" called Greta, and the dog bounded away.

"You were really picking it," Alex said between sips of soda. "Did you make an error today?"

Jamie shook his head.

"You're still the best fielder in town," Alex said. "Let's see that glove."

"Let's see that soda." Jamie grinned.

The boys traded. Jamie took a long, cool drink as Alex flexed the glove a few times.

"The golden glove," Alex said smiling. "My man Jamie's got the golden glove."

THREE

"Jamie, Alex, you guys want to play some hoops?" Greta stood at the edge of the basketball court, with a basketball on her hip. Jason Kemp, Tony Lena, and Alan Weinberg stood behind her, milling around beneath one of the baskets.

"Come on," she said. "You guys will make it three on three. Two on two is boring. And besides, I'm sick of beating these guys."

Jamie and Alex traded glances. They were tired from the baseball game, but they both had the same response. "Sure," they said.

Greta turned and dribbled slowly toward the basket. "How about Jamie, Alex, and Tony against us three?" she suggested. "Straight sixteen. Winners out. Clear everything. I'll shoot for outs."

Jamie nodded as he sized up the opposing players.

Greta feathered a fifteen-foot jump shot that hit nothing but net.

"Our ball," she said.

"I'll cover Jason," Jamie said, motioning to the tall seventh grader.

The game started poorly for Jamie's team. Greta hit a few quick baskets and Jason dominated the backboards.

During one play, Jamie cut for the basket, but fumbled a perfect pass from Alex out of bounds.

"Too bad you can't wear your glove playing hoops," Alex teased.

But slowly Jamie's team climbed back into the game. Jamie and Alex started hitting their shots, and Tony tightened up the defense on Greta.

"What's the count?" Alex asked.

"9–7, us," Greta answered.

Jamie took a pass from Tony and slipped the ball back to the streaking guard for a layup on a perfect give-and-go.

9–8.

But Greta got hot again from the outside,

popping in three straight jumpers. 12–8.

"Come on, Tony," Alex said, slamming the ball to the court. "You gotta cover Gretzky. She's killing us. You want to switch?"

"No way, man," Tony shot back angrily. "Chill out and play."

Alex darted out and stole a pass and hit a quick jump shot. Tony nailed a running hook shot. Then Jamie drove the lane for a twisting scoop shot that touched off the backboard and dropped through the net.

"YES!"

"12–11. Comeback time." The game was heating up.

Tony flicked a quick pass toward Jamie cutting for the basket. Jason tipped the ball as Jamie streaked by. The ball bounced out of bounds.

"Our ball," Alex said quickly.

Jamie shook his head and tapped his chest with his fingertips.

"I touched it before it went out," said Jamie. "It's their ball."

Alex spread his arms out wide, hopelessly looking at the sky and laughing.

"Why do you have to be so honest?" he asked. "It's 12–11. Be honest when it's 3–2. All right, their ball."

The teams traded baskets.

"What's the count?" Alex asked again.

"14–13, us," Greta answered. "Our ball."

Greta sent up an off-balance jumper that rattled around the rim and fell out. Tony got the rebound and flipped a quick pass to Jamie, whose long shot swished through the net. The score was 14–14.

"Clutch hoop."

"Prime-time player, baby."

"Jay-mee!" a voice echoed from the top of the hill. Jamie looked up and saw his mother standing there with her hands cupped around her mouth.

"Jamie," she called. "Dinnertime."

"Just two more baskets, Mom?" Jamie pleaded.

"It's six o'clock and dinner's ready right now!" she shouted.

Jamie looked around desperately.

"How about next basket wins?" he suggested to the other players.

"No way," said Greta. "You guys got the ball."

"Jay-mee!"

"All right, I'm coming, Mom," Jamie yelled toward the figure on the hill, flipping the ball to Alan Weinberg. "Your ball, next basket wins."

Alan passed to Jason who surprised Jamie by spinning quickly toward the basket. Tony slid over to help out, but Jason slipped a pass to Greta spotting up in the corner. Jamie jumped out at Greta.

"Gretzky!" he screamed, hoping to distract her shot.

Too late. Jamie turned to watch the ball's easy arc to the rim. Swish.

Jamie's face twisted into a pained expression and his shoulders sank.

"James Michael Bennett, get up here or I'll come down there and get you!"

Jamie turned. "See you guys later," he said as he ran up the hill in the gathering darkness.

FOUR

Clear your places," Carolyn Bennett said with a wave of her hand. Jamie and his nine-year-old brother, Brad, got up and took their plates to the kitchen sink.

Brad opened the refrigerator. "Is there any more of that chocolate cake, Mom?" he asked.

"No, but you can have some yogurt," she answered. Brad closed the refrigerator door.

"What time is Dad coming home?" Jamie asked.

"Later. He played golf with Mr. Widder this afternoon. He said they would probably eat dinner at the golf course."

"I hope he'll be home soon," Jamie said

eagerly. "I want to tell him about the baseball and basketball games today."

"How did the baseball game go?"

"Great! The glove—"

Jamie's words stuck in his throat. The glove! He had left it back at the park. Jamie could have kicked himself. He was *always* forgetting and losing things. He did not want his mother to find out that he had left his golden glove behind.

"How was the glove?" Mrs. Bennett asked, sipping her coffee.

"Great," Jamie said, quickly running through his mind all the places he might have left the precious leather. *The dugout. The soda machine. The fence. That's it,* Jamie thought. *The fence. I left it there when Alex and I went to play hoops.*

"It should be great the way you oiled it all winter," Jamie's mom continued. "I wish you would take care of all of your things that well."

Mrs. Bennett got up from the table. "I'll get the dishes," she said. "You boys go on upstairs and get that room straightened up before bedtime. It's getting pretty messy in there."

Jamie and Brad scrambled upstairs.

"Hey, Jamie," said Brad, pausing outside their room. "Think I could play baseball next time you guys get together?"

"I don't know, Brad. Most of the kids are older. It's fast-pitch."

"Who played?"

"Lots of kids. The Porters and their crowd. Alex. Some of the kids who made the All-Star team last year. I didn't see any nine-year-olds there."

"Nine and a half," Brad corrected.

"Listen, Brad," Jamie said as the boys entered their room. "Will you do me a big favor?"

"Depends."

"Could you start picking up the room? I gotta do something."

"Okay," said Brad, eyeing Jamie. "What's up?"

Jamie lowered his voice to a whisper. "I left my glove down at the field," he said. "I don't want Mom and Dad to find out I forgot it."

"Okay." Brad nodded. "But you better find it quick, or they're gonna kill you. Remember when you lost that hooded sweatshirt?"

"I know," said Jamie grimly. "Thanks."

Jamie tiptoed down the stairs and peeked down the hall to the kitchen. His mother was sweeping the floor. An oldies station played a Beatles tune in the background.

Jamie slowly turned the knob on the front door and quietly pushed the screen door open. Taking a deep breath, he silently closed the doors and stepped out into the night.

A sliver of a spring moon hung in the sky. The streetlight at the top of the hill and the lights of the tennis courts splashed long black shadows across the park.

Jamie carefully edged his way down the darkened hill to the park. When he reached flat ground, he ran across the basketball court to the outfield fence where he and Alex had shared the postgame soda. Jamie felt along the dark edge of the fence. The grass was cool and damp from the night air.

Nothing.

Jamie got down on his hands and knees and crawled along the bottom edge of the wooden fence, groping the darkness with his hands.

Still nothing.

Finally, Jamie sat with his knees tucked against his chin and the hard wood of the outfield fence against his back. The light from the tennis courts cast an eerie glow. The air was chilled, with only the barest hint of spring. The tennis courts were empty.

Jamie's glove was gone.

FIVE

"You sure you left it here?" Alex asked, squinting into the bright sun.

"Sure. Don't you remember?" Jamie said, pacing the edge of the outfield fence. "We were sitting here yesterday having a soda and then Gretzky asked if we wanted to play three on three. I put my glove down and that was the last time I saw it."

Alex nodded and looked around.

Jamie, still pacing, moaned, "Mom and Dad are going to be so mad. I'm always losing things. And I'm gonna hear about every one of them. My sweatshirt. My watch. That basketball from last Christmas."

"The Red Sox T-shirt," Alex added. "The K-2 football…"

"Come on, Alex. Give me a break. Don't

make me feel worse," Jamie said. "What am I going to do about my glove?"

Alex brightened. "You didn't *lose* your glove, Jamie. I mean it didn't just get up and walk away. Somebody must have taken it. All we gotta do is figure out who took it before your parents find out."

"That better be quick, Alex. Practice starts next Saturday and opening day is the week after that."

"Hey!" a voice shouted from the baseball diamond. "You guys want to play? We're picking teams."

Alex looked at Jamie. "You want to?"

"I don't have a glove."

"You can use mine. I'll borrow from somebody else. Come on. It'll cheer you up."

The kids gathered around the pitcher's mound. Once again the Porter brothers presented their demands.

"Billy and I gotta play together," Danny Porter said, his arms folded tight across his chest.

"Again?" Alex shouted. "What are you guys, attached at the hip or something?"

Everyone laughed but the Porters.

"Danny and I play together, wise guy," Billy said, staring straight at Alex. "You can have first two picks just like yesterday."

"And we'll beat you just like yesterday."

"Beat us? No way!"

"It was 39–38," Alex said with a smile. "I was keeping score in my head, right Jamie?"

"I think the score was 39–37," Jamie corrected him.

"Chill out and pick," Danny Porter said with a wave of his hand.

"Jamie and Adam."

"Hey, we want Adam!"

"Chill out and pick," Alex mocked.

After the final player was chosen, Billy Porter said, "We got first ups."

Jamie trudged out to shortstop. Though Alex's glove looked like Jamie's, it felt different, almost strange, on his hand.

The first batter, Danny Porter, stepped to the plate and took his practice swings.

"Are you sure you don't need your brother to help you bat?" Alex teased from his position at third base.

Danny glared at Alex and slapped a hard hopper right at Jamie. The ball took a funny bounce at the end, hit off the heel of the borrowed glove and skittered away. Jamie grabbed the ball bare-handed, but held up his throw as he looked up to see Danny Porter race across the bag.

"Bad bounce," Alex said as Jamie flipped the ball back to the pitcher.

"So what happened, hot shot?" Danny Porter shouted from first base. "You're not so great without your glove."

Jamie's mind wandered back to the missing glove. *How could he have lost something so important?* The crack of Billy Porter's bat startled him into action. Jamie sprinted to his left and reached out for the skipping grounder. The ball slapped off the glove and angled out into right field. Running all the way, Danny Porter slid into third. As Danny dusted himself off, he said to Alex in a voice loud enough for Jamie to hear, "Another error on the shortstop, Alex. You'd better move that guy to right field."

The game continued, with players coming and going and no one but Alex and the Porter brothers even trying to keep score. Jamie's fielding was a mixed bag. He made some plays and muffed some others, but the magic of the day before was lost.

Later, Jamie and Alex leaned against the same outfield fence sharing a soda. Once again, Mingo ran up to the boys, his tongue and tail wagging.

"I think he wants some of the soda," Jamie laughed.

"Okay, Mingo. Here you go." Alex tilted the can and let a slow stream of soda spill onto Mingo's tongue and Mingo slurped it up with sloppy delight. "That's all you're getting."

"Tough game," Alex said, watching Mingo race away. "You had some tough chances."

"I've made harder plays before," Jamie answered, pounding a fist into Alex's glove.

Jamie took the glove off and tossed it to his buddy.

"Sorry, but your glove just didn't feel right," he said.

Alex shrugged. "Least we found out one thing."

"Yeah," Jamie laughed sadly, "that I better find my glove fast."

"Nope," said Alex confidently. "That the Porters stole it."

"What?" Jamie scrunched up his face as he stared at his friend. "How do you figure that?"

"Remember what Danny yelled from first base after you booted that grounder? He said you weren't so hot without your glove. Well, how'd he know you didn't have your glove unless he took it?"

Jamie shook his head. "You're crazy, man. He probably saw me borrowing your glove."

"My glove looks pretty much the same as yours," Alex said, holding his glove up to Jamie's eyes. "Anyway, I hate those Porter guys. They're always bossing everyone around."

"That doesn't mean they'd steal things," Jamie said, taking the soda from Alex.

"Maybe, maybe not," Alex said, looking

from side to side. "But I know a way to find out."

"How?"

"Easy. Tomorrow after school we'll head over to their house."

"What?" Jamie said, almost laughing. "The Porters are just gonna hand me back my glove?"

"No, stupid. They got a big garage where they keep their sports stuff. We'll just go in and take a look around. I'll bet you that's where it is."

"If those guys catch us, they'll pound us," Jamie said, handing the soda to Alex.

Alex shook his head. "They won't catch us. They go to Tower School. They get out about twenty minutes after us."

Alex lifted the soda can straight up and emptied it in a big gulp.

"Hey, I wanted some!" Jamie protested, grabbing the can. "You drank the whole thing."

Alex fended off his friend with a raised elbow. "I figured out the mystery," he said. "I get the last swig."

"So what about the mystery. I still don't have my glove."

Alex patted Jamie on the shoulder. "Don't worry, Jamie. We'll have that golden glove of yours back before the Porters step off the school bus tomorrow," Alex said.

SIX

Jamie's heart pounded as he pedaled his bike through the streets of his hometown.

Alex raced ahead.

"Come on," he said, looking back at Jamie. "Hurry up. We don't have much time."

Jamie put his head down and pushed harder on the pedals. His mind was racing as fast as his bike: *What if the Porters caught them? What if the Porters' parents caught them? What if the garage was locked? What if the Porters had a dog? What if the Porters had a BIG dog? What if the glove wasn't there?*

"Come on Jamie," called Alex, waving his arm in a circle. "It's right around the corner."

The boys took a wide corner at top speed and skidded to a stop.

"There it is," Alex said, pointing to a large home with a two-car garage set back from the street.

"Let's ditch the bikes here," suggested Jamie, trying to catch his breath.

The boys hid their bikes behind the bushes along the sidewalk. They walked quickly toward the Porters' house.

At the end of the Porters' driveway, Jamie grabbed Alex's arm.

"I don't know, Alex, this doesn't feel right. It's like we're breaking into their house or something."

"We're just going into their garage to get the glove they stole from you."

"I know, but it feels like we're the guys doing the stealing."

"You want your glove back, don't you?" asked Alex impatiently.

"Of course I do," said Jamie. He let go of Alex's arm and looked all around, afraid of whom or what he might see.

Jamie and Alex walked up the driveway

and peered into the garage through a window clouded with dust.

"No cars," said Alex. "Let's go." Jamie grabbed Alex's arm again.

"You wait outside as a lookout and watch for the bus," Jamie said. "It's my glove. I'll be able to recognize it faster."

When Alex lifted the garage door, the rusty hinges squeaked and groaned. Jamie crawled under the door and peered into the dark space. "Make it fast," Alex said.

The middle of the garage was cool and empty, like a cave. Slowly Jamie's eyes adjusted to the dim light and he looked around. Bikes, lawn chairs, garbage barrels, and tools were shoved along the walls. Jamie moved among the mess, searching for someplace where the glove might be.

"You see anything?" Alex called.

"Not yet."

"Hurry up!"

Just then, Jamie spied a large covered box in the corner near a door leading to the house. He opened the box and his heart jumped. The box was piled high with sports equipment. Basketballs, baseball hats, hockey sticks were all in a jumble.

"Hey, I think I found something," Jamie called out in a hoarse whisper.

"Hurry up, man, that bus should be showing up any minute," Alex said.

Jamie reached in and rummaged around in the box. He pulled out a pair of baseball gloves and examined them frantically. An Albert Pujols model. A Grady Sizemore model. Both had the name Porter scrawled in marker across one of the fingers.

Jamie kept looking inside the box. No more gloves. He tossed the Porters' baseball gloves back into the box and closed the top.

"Oh no!" Alex shouted.

Jamie looked up to see Alex scrambling into the garage.

"What are you doing?" Jamie asked in a panic.

"The Porters are coming."

"Let's get out of here," said Jamie, quickly trying to duck under the door.

Alex grabbed Jamie by the arm, pulled him back in, and let the garage door fall.

"No," he hissed. "They'll see us for sure. Let's wait."

"Why didn't you warn me sooner?" Jamie whispered.

"I was looking back at you and the bus just came zooming around the corner."

"Shhh," Jamie said, jerking his finger to his lips. The boys crouched in the corner of the garage. *I knew we should never have come in here,* Jamie thought, his heart pounding.

Jamie could hear voices from inside the house. Footsteps. Voices. A door slamming. More voices. Finally, loud music blared out.

Alex whispered, "We can't stay here forever. We better make our move while the music's on."

Jamie cocked his head toward the garage door. The two boys tiptoed across the garage floor.

"Just lift the door up high enough so I can slip under," Jamie whispered.

Alex lifted the door. Jamie flattened out and slipped across the cool cement floor. Jamie held the door as Alex crawled out.

"Let's go," Alex said in a loud, panicked whisper.

Jamie let the door slip. He was halfway across the lawn when he heard the door fall shut. The two boys hopped on their bikes and hurried down the street.

A few blocks away, they began to coast.

"Do you think they heard us?" Alex asked breathlessly.

"No," Jamie answered, shaking his head. "They couldn't hear anything over that music."

"Yeah," Alex laughed. "Long live rock music!" Alex reared back his head and let out his best rock-star howl. Jamie joined in laughing and singing through the streets.

"You didn't see the glove?" Alex asked finally.

"Nah, just their stuff. I don't think they took it, Alex. I mean, why would they steal my glove?"

"Jerks like them don't need a reason," Alex said, as the boys slowed down for a stoplight.

"Looks like you're gonna have to tell your

mom and dad," Alex said as each boy leaned on one foot waiting for the light to turn green.

"Yeah, I know," said Jamie, staring at the light. "You know, I think I'd rather get pounded by the Porters."

Seven

o how was school today?" Jamie's dad, Jack Bennett, asked, looking up from his dinner.

"Okay," Jamie answered as he pushed his chicken nuggets about with his fork.

"What's today, Thursday? Did you have computer lab today?"

"Yeah, we played a new math game."

"How did you do?"

"Okay, I guess."

"Jamie, don't play with your food," his mom said.

"I ate two. Do I have to eat the last two?"

"Yes, you do." His mother frowned.

"When does baseball practice start for you guys?" Jamie's dad asked.

Jamie looked across the table to Brad. Brad knew that after several days of trying to summon his courage, Jamie planned to tell his parents about his lost baseball glove tonight.

"Saturday," Jamie said. He looked over at Brad and their eyes locked for a few seconds. Brad looked down at his plate and Jamie looked over to his dad. "This Saturday," Jamie added, trying to cover up the nervousness he felt.

"How are the Giants going to be this year?"

"Okay, I guess," he said. Jamie lowered his head and stared absentmindedly at his plate. "Um, Dad. Mom..." he said softly, so softly that his parents didn't hear him.

"Is Mr. McKenna going to coach you again this year, James?" his mother asked.

"Yeah, I guess so."

"Can I have dessert?" Brad asked, pushing his chair back.

"Not until everyone is finished," his father reminded him.

"Mom, Dad..." Jamie began again.

"May I be excused?" Brad asked as he stood up from the table.

"What's your hurry?" his dad asked.

"Mom, Dad," Jamie repeated, trying to get up the nerve to say what he knew he had to say.

"I'll clear my place," Brad announced quickly. He didn't want to stay for the fireworks.

"Sit down," Mr. Bennett said impatiently. "Wait until everyone is finished, then you can clear the dishes."

Brad plopped back in his chair like a sack of stones. Jamie cleared his throat. "Mom, Dad, I've got something to tell you about baseball."

Jamie's parents looked at each other and then at him.

"I think I...I'm pretty sure I...um, lost my glove."

"What? Your new glove? How could you lose your glove?" Jamie's dad thundered.

"Oh, Jamie...," his mother sighed.

"May I go do my homework? I've really got a lot," Brad asked hopefully.

"No, Brad. Be quiet," his father answered. "What happened, Jamie? Where do you think you lost it?"

"At the park."

"When?"

"Saturday."

"How?"

"I forgot to bring it home after playing basketball."

"Have you looked for it?"

"Yes. I love that glove," Jamie said, trying to fight back tears. Now he wished his father would let Brad leave the table. "I looked everywhere." He decided not to mention that he had even looked in the Porters' garage. He kept that secret to himself.

Jack Bennett put his hand to his head, like he was getting a headache, and stared at his plate. After a long silence, he looked up and said, "You'll just have to play without a glove."

"Without a glove?" Jamie blurted. "But, Dad..."

"Jack, maybe Jamie could earn the money for a new glove?" his mom suggested.

"Do you know how much a new glove like that costs? About $100!"

"Jack...," Jamie's mother started.

"No, Carolyn," said Jamie's father. "He has to learn to take care of his things. He loses everything!"

Oh no, Jamie thought, *here comes the list*.

"He lost that hooded sweatshirt, the basketball he got from Grandpa for Christmas, his watch, that little football..."

"That Red Sox T-shirt," Brad chimed in.

"Shut up!" Jamie yelled at his little brother.

"You're excused, Bradley," Mr. Bennett said sternly. "This does not concern you." With that, Brad scrambled away from the table.

"I can't play without a glove, Dad," Jamie pleaded. "It's probably against the rules and anyway this is a big year for me. I could be one of the best fielders in the league this year."

Jamie's dad shook his head.

"You'll just have to find another one. Maybe Alex has an extra. Or you can borrow a glove from one of your friends. But we are not buying you another one. Period."

Jamie swallowed hard.

"Jamie, why don't you go upstairs," his mom said gently.

Jamie got up and walked slowly to his room. He closed his bedroom door behind him and grabbed a baseball off his dresser. He sat on the edge of his bed flipping the ball from one hand to another.

Brad opened the door and poked his head into the room. "Sorry about the crack about the Red Sox shirt. That was dumb."

"You got that right," said Jamie as he looked at Brad. But he wasn't really mad at Brad and Brad could tell.

"Think Mom will get Dad to get you a new glove?"

Jamie shook his head. "Nah," he said. "Dad is really mad. He's doesn't usually change his mind when he's that mad."

Brad tossed Jamie the baseball glove that he had been holding behind his back. "Wanna try mine?" he asked.

Jamie squeezed his hand into Brad's

glove and slapped the baseball into the pocket. “Thanks, but it’s really too small. I need something bigger.”

Brad shrugged and sat down beside his brother on the edge of the bed.

Jamie flopped back against the covers of the bed. “What am I gonna do without a glove?” he moaned.

“Hey,” Brad said. “My friend Paul’s got a bunch of older brothers. Maybe one of them has an extra glove you can borrow.”

“I don’t want to borrow a glove. I want my own glove back,” said Jamie.

“Maybe Mom can convince Dad to buy me a new one,” Brad suggested. “Just make it a little bigger than I need.”

Jamie smiled but said, “I think Dad would see right through that.”

The boys sat and thought some more. Their thinking was interrupted by a knock on the door. Jamie propped himself up on his elbows and saw his mother enter the room. One look at her expression and he knew.

No glove.

Eight

The next day, Jamie and Brad stood at the door of a large, rambling house. Brad rang the doorbell. A teenager wearing a backwards baseball cap and headphones opened the door.

"Is Paul home?" Brad asked.

"Paul! Company!" the boy shouted, walking away from the opened door.

A stocky, dark-haired boy about Brad's age bounded down the steps, dressed in an oversized black T-shirt.

"Hey, Paul."

"Hey, Brad. What's up?"

"My brother Jamie lost his baseball glove, and we were wondering if he could borrow one of yours for the season."

"Yeah, sure. But why don't your mom and dad buy you a new one?" Paul asked looking at Jamie.

"I'm always losing stuff," Jamie answered. "I guess they want to teach me a lesson or something."

Paul nodded as if he understood the way moms and dads were, then said, "We got a lot of sports stuff downstairs. We probably got an old glove."

The three boys walked to the back of the house and descended a narrow stairway. Paul flicked on a light switch. The light revealed a large, messy basement. Half of the basement was a laundry room, stacked high with piles of dirty clothes. The other half was a playroom with a sofa, a Ping-Pong table, and a wide assortment of sports equipment strewn about.

"Man!" said Jamie letting out a whistle. "You guys got more sports stuff than Pete's Sports Shop. How many kids in your family?"

"Five. I got three brothers and one sister. I'm the youngest. We all play sports."

Paul opened a closet door and started pulling out even more sports equipment.

"Try this one," Paul said, tossing a weather-worn baseball mitt at Jamie.

Jamie slipped the glove onto his left hand. The glove was about the right size, but the leather was stiff, flat, and lifeless. Jamie smacked his fist a few times into what was left of the pocket. When Jamie tried to snap the glove shut, the leather, long forgotten in the closet, groaned into place.

"That was my brother Greg's Little League glove. He's in college now."

"Seems kinda crummy," Brad observed. "Got anything else?"

Paul kept looking, tossing out a couple more candidates for Jamie to inspect. The gloves were either too small or in worse shape than the first.

Jamie kept pounding his fist into the pocket of the first glove. He licked his fingers and rubbed the spit into the leather.

"What do you think?" Brad asked finally.

Jamie looked up at Paul. "You think your

brother will want anything for it?" Jamie asked.

"Nah," said Paul, shaking his head. "You can keep it. Greg won't even know it's gone."

Jamie and Brad walked home in silence. Jamie kept flexing the glove and trying to work a pocket into the leather with his fists.

When they arrived home, Brad asked, "Do you want to play catch?"

"Sure. Go get your glove and a baseball."

Brad was back in a flash. As he burst out the front door, he flipped a quick throw. Jamie reached easily to his left to catch the ball. The ball hit the middle of the old mitt. Jamie tried to squeeze the glove shut, but the ball squirmed loose and plunked to the ground.

NINE

"All right, kids, bring it in," Mr. McKenna shouted. The boys and girls of the Giants hustled in from the outfield where they had been warming up by tossing baseballs back and forth.

"Take a knee, kids." Mr. McKenna stood above the team. He was a tall man, with a baseball cap pushed back on his head, his eyes squinting in the afternoon sun.

"Okay, we're going to start with some infield and then take some BP."

"We gonna scrimmage, Mr. Mac?" asked Sharon Hanley, the Giants second baseman.

"We'll try to if you guys look good in practice. I'm going to try different people in different positions. But I'm looking for the best defense we can put out on the field because..." Mr. McKenna paused, waiting for a familiar answer.

"Defense wins games!" the Giants shouted back.

"All right." Mr. McKenna smiled and then went down the lineup. "Alex at third. Jamie at short. Sharon on second. Will at first. Andy, Theresa, and Zack in the outfield. Tommy, you're catching.

"The rest of you kids are running bases. Don't take off until the ball is hit. Let's go."

The Giants clapped their hands and ran out to their positions. Jamie kept pounding and flexing his glove nervously, hoping to loosen up the leather.

"Okay, Alex. Look alive." Mr. McKenna, holding a 29-inch bat in his right hand. He flipped a baseball up with his left and slapped a hard one-hopper to third. Alex stepped in, caught the ball waist high, and pegged a strike to the first baseman.

"All right. Another."

Alex fielded the next grounder with equal ease.

"Okay, Jamie, here's a hot one."

Mr. McKenna smacked a grass-cutter to Jamie's left. Jamie darted a few quick steps, reached out his glove, but only knocked the ball down. Jamie quickly picked the ball up with his bare hand and fired to first. Too late. The runner was safe.

"Another."

This time, Mr. McKenna sent a bouncer right at Jamie that Jamie had to play on an in-between hop. The ball hit the heel of Jamie's battered mitt, knocked off his chest, and fell a few feet in front of him. Safe all around.

"Second and first. Force at every base but home. Remember, get the easy out," Mr. McKenna reminded the infield.

Another grounder bounced out to Jamie. Jamie fumbled the ball, but he recovered it in time to flip it to Sharon covering second.

"Good play," Mr. McKenna said in an encouraging voice. "That's just how to stay with it."

Jamie kicked the dirt as he returned to short.

"Take it easy, man," Alex called from third

base in a low voice. "You made the play."

"Yeah," Jamie said. "Third time never fails."

"Wake up, Jamie," Mr. McKenna called. "Got a force at second. Let's get two."

The coach cracked a hard grounder to second. Sharon Hanley glided easily to her right, fielded the ball cleanly, and tossed it to second where Jamie was covering the bag. Jamie caught the ball and touched the bag with his right foot as he swept across and fired to first.

"Double play!"

"4–6–3."

"Way to go, Sharon."

"Great throw, Jamie."

Practice continued into the afternoon. The Giants finished fielding practice. Then everyone got a turn at bat.

Jamie felt great at the plate. He sprayed hard line shots all over the ballyard. But in the field it was another story. Jamie struggled throughout the entire practice, fumbling grounders and never quite feeling at home at shortstop.

After a short scrimmage, Mr. McKenna ended practice by calling the team together.

"Good job, kids. Practice on Wednesday at six. Next Saturday is opening day. Be sure to play catch whenever you can. Get your mom, dad, anybody. Just throw that ball around. See you Wednesday."

Jamie and Alex got a soda from the machine and sat with their backs against the outfield fence facing the basketball courts.

"Wonder where Gretzky is?" Alex said, glancing at the empty hardtop.

Jamie shrugged and handed the soda to Alex.

"I don't know," Jamie said. "Maybe she's sick or something."

"Man, that girl's gotta be dead not to be working on her jump shot."

Alex took a gulp of soda and then said, "Everybody looked a bit rusty out there."

"Yeah, especially me," Jamie said in a soft voice.

"You made some plays," Alex protested.

"Missed some, too. The way things are

going, I may end up with a higher batting average than fielding average."

"Yeah, you were really stinging the ball. How's the glove?"

"I don't know," Jamie said, sounding discouraged. "It just doesn't feel right. Still feels kind of stiff. I wish I could find the other one."

Alex took a swig of soda. "Your golden glove is long gone, man. Looks like you're stuck with that old one."

Jamie's chin sank into his chest.

"Why don't you go down to Pete's Sports Shop?" Alex suggested to his buddy. "Maybe he's got something to help loosen up the leather."

"Yeah, you're right," Jamie said, pulling his hat down low to shield his eyes from the sinking afternoon sun.

TEN

A small bell jingled above his head as Jamie opened the door to Pete's Sports Shop. The late afternoon sun slanted through the front store window and cast an orange glow into the crowded little shop.

Inside, Greta Pemberton sat next to her mother, lacing up a new pair of sneakers.

"I hope these last, Pete," Greta's mom said. "She wears them out before she outgrows them."

Greta got up and bounced on her shoes like a restless fighter waiting for the bell.

"Hey, Gretzky," Jamie said. "Nice shoes."

"Hey, Jamie," Greta smiled, looking at her sneakers and then at Jamie.

Pete Bikakis stood up. He was a trim, bald man with close-cropped gray hair along the sides of his head. Although Pete was in his eighties, he didn't look that old to Jamie. He still moved with the ease of an athlete.

As he waited, Jamie fingered the baseball gloves that hung on the wall. He shook his head when he saw the price tags. *Man*, he thought, *I'd have to do chores for a year to earn the money to buy one of these things.*

"See you at the park, Jamie," Greta called out as she left the store with her new sneakers slung over her shoulder.

"See ya around, Gretzky."

"How can I help you, Jamie?" Pete asked as he walked across the store.

"Actually, Pete, it's my glove that needs help," Jamie said, showing Pete the old leather mitt.

"This isn't the one you bought last spring."

"No, I lost that one."

Pete shook his head sympathetically. "Ooh. Lost your gamer, Jamie. That's too bad."

"Gamer? What do you mean, gamer?"

"You know, the glove you use in the game. Lots of the pros have a bunch of gloves they are breaking in. But a ballplayer usually only has one gamer."

"Really?"

"Sure," Pete continued. "A player takes special care of his gamer." The old man put out his hand. "Let's take a look at that glove of yours."

Jamie handed the glove over. Pete stretched the glove out, carefully inspecting each part. Jamie watched the old man's hands skillfully move over the mitt. Pete's hands were so tough and leathery that it was hard to tell his skin from the glove.

"This one isn't so bad. Leather's in pretty good shape. Laces aren't frayed. How's it treating you?"

Jamie shook his head. "I don't know. I'm borrowing it from someone until I find mine. It feels kinda stiff—not like the one I had. That one was perfect."

"Well," said Pete, handing the glove back to Jamie. "You gotta break this one in all over again."

"How do I do that?" Jamie asked. "First game is in a week."

"You can use that neat's-foot oil I gave you last fall and work it into the pocket, but ballplayers use all kinds of stuff to break in their gloves."

"Like what?"

Pete laughed and scratched his chin. "Some players soak their glove in warm water. I read once where Robin Yount used to throw his glove into a Jacuzzi and then let it dry out. Must have worked. Yount was the American League's Most Valuable Player in the 1980s as a shortstop and again as a center fielder."

Jamie smiled. "We don't have a Jacuzzi, Pete."

"Well, some players use shaving cream instead of oil," old Pete continued. "They just lather up the pocket. But the player with the weirdest method was Eddie Brinkman, a great fielding shortstop back in the 1960s and 70s who couldn't hit a lick. He used to pour hot coffee onto his glove."

"Hot coffee?" Jamie repeated, amazed.

"With cream and sugar," Pete said with a

wink. "But don't try that. Stick with neat's-foot oil. I don't want your mother coming down here saying I filled your head with crazy ideas."

"I don't think anything will help this glove," Jamie said with a discouraged voice. "It's just too old and stiff, and, well, I just can't field with it."

Pete smiled around the corners of his mouth and shook his head ever so slightly. He turned to the woman behind the cash register and said, "Mrs. Wyman, could you watch the store for a while? I'll be in the back room." Then he motioned to Jamie as he walked to the back of the store.

"Come on," Pete said. "I want to show you something."

ELEVEN

Pete clicked a switch and a series of overhead lights came on to brighten the small, crowded room. A long, wooden workbench covered with tools, baseballs, and baseball gloves sat flush against the back wall. All sorts of baseball bats, hockey sticks, and other equipment were angled in the corners. Above the workbench a half dozen or so baseball gloves hung on wooden pegs. The air smelled of oil, leather, and wood.

Pete looked around proudly. "This is my office," he said. "I come back here and work on some of the equipment, especially the gloves. I always liked fixing things better than selling things."

"What are those?" Jamie asked, pointing to the gloves on the wall.

"That's what I wanted to show you."

Pete reached up and pulled what looked to be two old padded work gloves off the first wooden peg and handed them to Jamie.

"Go ahead and put them on. They may be a bit big, but go ahead."

Jamie slipped his hands into the hard brown leather. The tops of his fingers poked through five holes in each glove.

"You know what those are?" Pete asked.

Jamie shook his head.

"Baseball gloves."

"Baseball gloves?" Jamie repeated in surprise. "When did they use these things?"

"Back in the 1870s and 1880s. Before that, ballplayers didn't even wear gloves. In fact, those were my grandfather's gloves. He played for the Philadelphia City Items. We found those in an attic trunk after he died."

"Why did they wear two?" Jamie asked, wiggling his fingers.

"The gloves were just to protect their hands. They wore two because they caught the ball with both hands. The holes left their fingers free so they could throw the ball."

Pete reached up and picked another glove off another peg.

"This one looks more like a glove," he observed.

Once again, Jamie slid his fingers into the flattened leather.

"Just looks like a bunch of padded fingers," Jamie said, pounding his fist into the glove. "Not much of a pocket. Where's the webbing?"

"The first baseball gloves didn't have any webbing."

"Was this your glove?" Jamie asked.

"No," Pete laughed. "I'm old, but not *that* old. That was one of my father's gloves. He played for a team called the Flint Vehicles before World War I."

"What did he play?"

"Mostly third base. Had a real good arm."

"How did he ever catch anything?" Jamie asked, trying to flex the clumsy mitt.

"They had their ways. A good fielder can learn to catch with any glove. You know what Honus Wagner said?"

"Honus Wagner?" Jamie asked. "Who's he?"

Pete's head snapped back in surprise. "Honus Wagner. Why, he was the Flying Dutchman," he said. "You play shortstop. You should know about the greatest shortstop who ever lived. He was one of the first five players voted into the National Baseball Hall of Fame. Along with Babe Ruth, Ty Cobb, Walter Johnson, and Christy Mathewson. That's pretty good company."

"When did he play?" Jamie asked.

"Back before World War I. Probably with a glove not much different from the one you're holding. Anyway, Honus Wagner said this: 'There ain't much to being a ballplayer, if you're a ballplayer.'"

"Maybe so, but it sure is easier to be a ballplayer if you've got a good glove."

"Ah," Pete exclaimed waving his hand at Jamie. "Let me get my glove."

Pete reached along the row of pegs to pull

another glove down. He lovingly rubbed the tips of his fingers along the well-worn pocket of the glove.

"This was my gamer back before World War II," he said, with a faraway kind of voice.

"You played?"

"Sure. Played shortstop. I was going to try out for the Kalamazoo Kazoos in 1941, but then I went into the Army. That was during World War II."

Pete tossed his gamer to Jamie. "That glove's played baseball in North Africa and Italy."

"Ever play pro?" Jamie asked, eyeing the glove.

"No, just semipro. Back then, everybody played—for towns, factories, businesses. And everybody knew how to play.

"I see kids down at Green Street Park," Pete continued, shaking his head at the memory. "They just stick their gloves down on the ground trying to get grounders."

"But isn't that the way you're supposed to do it?"

"No!" Pete thundered. "You scoop up a grounder. Grab your glove and let me show you."

Pete and Jamie put on their gloves and stepped out into a small, fenced yard in back of the shop. Pete motioned Jamie to one side of the yard and tossed him an easy grounder. Jamie stuck out his glove and snagged it easily.

"No!" Pete walked across the yard and stood next to Jamie. "Don't just plop your glove down," he instructed. "You move over and try to get in front of the ball. Like this." Pete demonstrated by scrambling across the yard low and quick like a crab on hot sand.

"Then when the ball gets to your glove, you bring your glove back and up." Pete slipped his hands back as if he were cradling a ball. "And then you're ready to throw. Let's see you do it, Jamie."

Pete walked back across the yard and started peppering Jamie with ground balls. He shouted encouragement as Jamie fielded grounder after grounder:

Move those feet.

Bring the hands back.

Keep the glove down.

Good. Cradle it. Imagine you're catching an egg.

That's it. That's it.

Finally, Pete called an end to the workout. Jamie was smiling as the two walked back into the shop.

"When's that first game, Jamie?"

"Next Saturday."

"The teams still parade through town behind the fire trucks?"

"Sure."

"Just oil up that glove every night and play plenty of catch. If you don't have anybody to play catch with, just throw a tennis ball against a wall or your front step."

"Will that help?"

"Sure," Pete said, nodding his head. "Tennis ball is a lot bouncier than a baseball. You gotta bring your hands back or the ball will jump right out of your glove."

Jamie nodded and slapped the pocket of his glove.

"You'll be fine, Jamie," Pete said gently. "Just remember, it's never been the glove that made the ballplayer. It's always been the other way around."

TWELVE

Thwack! The bright green tennis ball smacked against the clapboard of the Bennett house. Jamie scooted to his right to get in front of the wildly bouncing ball. He scooped the ball back and up in an easy, graceful motion and threw hard.

Thwack!

Over and over Jamie threw the ball against the house and scrambled after the grounder. Each time Jamie concentrated on bringing his hands back while scooping up the grounder, just as Pete had instructed.

Thwack!

Another grounder.

Another scoop of the ball.

Another throw.

Thwack!

The early spring sun was sinking quietly. Jamie paused to take a long cool drink from a squeeze bottle he had set against the back fence. Wiping his mouth with the back of his glove, Jamie glanced over the fence to the field below. The field was freshly lined and mowed, ready for tomorrow's opening-day games.

Jamie was ready too. Or at least he hoped he was ready.

Every night for the past week, Jamie had rubbed oil into the pocket of the old glove. Then he'd placed a baseball in the mitt, tied a shoelace tight around the glove, and shoved the glove under his mattress. Every day, Jamie raced home after school and pulled the glove out from under the mattress for a practice session with either the back of his house or his brother Brad.

Jamie's mother had complained one time about the constant pounding on the back of the house. And one evening Jamie saw his father checking for loose shingles. A hard rain had cancelled the weekday practice.

But nothing had kept Jamie from practicing at home.

"Hi, Jamie," said Jamie's father as he rounded the corner of the house. "Getting ready for tomorrow?"

"Just fielding a few grounders," Jamie answered.

"How's the glove?"

"Feels pretty good. Feels better every time I use it."

"That's good. I ran into Mr. McKenna and he gave me something you might be interested in." Jamie's father handed Jamie a yellow card that had been folded in fourths.

"All right! The rosters and schedules!" Jamie said excitedly as he checked the card for the Giants roster.

GIANTS

Coach: Terry McKenna

PLAYER	AGE
James Bennett	12
Sharon Hanley	12
Alex Hammond	12
Thomas Lancaster	12
Theresa Thomas	12
Manuel Andujar	11
Michael Baker	11
Adam Kinner	11
William Feldman	11
Amanda Goodman	11
Andrew Locke	11
Tyler Phelps	11
Zachary Campbell	10
Joseph Symcak	10

"Who are you playing tomorrow?" Jamie's father asked as Jamie continued to study the roster.

"The Braves."

"How are they?"

Jamie glanced at the Braves roster.

BRAVES
Coach: John Young

PLAYER	AGE
Ellen Cooper	12
Jay Crandall	12
Max Eisenberg	12
Edmundo Gonzales	12
William Porter	12
Susan Young	12
Bradley Anderson	11
Anthony Bonuccelli	11
Brian Foster	11
Blair Johnston	11
Andrew Wong	11
Elizabeth Briggs	10
Patrick Farnsworth	10
Matthew Young	10

"They're tough. They got Billy Porter and a couple of other real good ballplayers, but we can beat them."

"When's the game?"

"We got the first game," Jamie said. "It should start around eleven o'clock in the morning."

"Good," Jamie's father answered. "Brad plays his first game at the minor-league field around two. Your mom and I want to see both."

Jamie's dad motioned to the house. "Let's see you field a couple," he said.

Jamie's father stood next to Jamie as he threw the ball against the house. *Thwack!*

"You know your mom almost talked me into buying you a new glove," he said.

Jamie kept throwing and his father kept talking.

"But I think you're getting old enough to understand that you have to take care of your things. You know, we can't run out to the store every time you lose something."

Jamie's father paused as Jamie scooped another grounder.

"You look pretty good with that glove," Jamie's father said. "Want to play catch?"

"Sure," Jamie said smiling.

Jamie's father ducked into the house and reappeared with his glove.

Without a word, Jamie and his father took up their familiar spots on two patches of worn grass in the Bennetts' backyard. They tossed the ball back and forth as they had done a thousand times before. From father to son. From son to father. A quiet game of catch in the dying evening light.

THIRTEEN

"Get in line," Mr. McKenna called out to the Giants, who were milling about nervously in the brilliant morning sunshine. "The parade is about to begin."

The Giants, dressed in burnt-orange hats and shirts and spanking white baseball pants, formed four rows and fell into the parade route along with the seven other baseball teams. Up ahead, the high school band started to play "Take Me Out to the Ballgame" and began to march forward in lockstep. Two fire engines draped in team banners followed the band. The teams, more or less in formation, marched behind the fire trucks.

The Braves were right in back of the Giants.

"Hey, Jamie," Billy Porter called to the front of the parade. "You better be ready to field some hot shots because we're gonna be hitting them your way. You too, Alex."

"Go ahead and try, Porter," Alex called back. "We'll be ready for you."

Billy just waved his glove and laughed.

"I can't stand that guy," Alex whispered angrily. "He's always bragging."

"He's just kidding around," Jamie said. "He's not bad."

"He stole your glove, didn't he?" Alex asked, glancing at Jamie.

Jamie looked straight ahead.

"I'm not so sure," he said.

The parade wound its way down the main street, through a sea of camcorders, cameras, and smiling faces.

As the Giants walked by Pete's Sports Shop, Jamie saw Pete in the doorway, waving. Pete caught Jamie's eye and quickly pantomimed a fielder scooping up a grounder. His throw ended with a wave of his hand.

As the teams marched on, Jamie reviewed in his mind Pete's fielding lesson: *Get in front of the ball. When it reaches your glove, bring your glove back and up and get ready to throw.*

When the teams reached the field and the parade was over, Mr. McKenna called the Giants together.

"Okay kids, opening day. Ready to go? We're up first.

"Here's the lineup. Theresa is leading off and playing center. Jamie's at short. Alex is at third. Tommy's catching and hitting cleanup. Manuel's in left. Sharon's at second and hitting sixth. Will's at first. Andy, you're on the mound and Zack, you're in right. I'll work in everybody else as the game goes along. Mike, you're the relief pitcher. Let's play smart and not give them any extra outs. Let's go."

Jamie stood on the on-deck circle with Theresa "Tessie" Thomas watching the Braves pitcher, Max Eisenberg, warm up.

"He looks a little wild, Tessie," Jamie observed. "Better look at a couple of pitches."

But Tessie did not take Jamie's advice. She struck out, nervously swinging at a series of bad pitches.

Jamie stepped into the batter's box. He stood in a slightly closed stance with the bat cocked behind his right ear.

The Braves pitcher was wild and high on the first two pitches. Jamie let them go by and found himself up in the count, two balls, no strikes.

He's gotta come in with one now, Jamie thought as he eyed the pitcher's windup. The next pitch was right down the center of the plate, and Jamie cracked a clean single over the shortstop's head.

The Giants bench exploded in cheers.

"All right!"

"Way to go, Jamie!"

Alex followed, slicing a curving liner down the right-field line. Jamie took off when he saw that the ball would bounce in fair territory. He rounded second and saw Amanda Goodman, the Giants third-base coach, windmilling her right arm, signaling Jamie to head home.

Jamie touched the bag and tore off for home plate. Tommy Lancaster, the Giants cleanup hitter, was in back of home plate, frantically pushing his hands palms down toward the ground.

"Slide, Jamie, slide!" Tommy screamed.

Jamie hit the dirt just as the ball landed in the catcher's mitt. Jamie felt the hard rubber of home plate slide beneath his spikes a split second before the catcher's mitt smacked his back. Safe!

The Giants bench was all backslaps.

"Let's keep it going, Tommy."

"Way to hit, Alex!"

"Rally time."

A walk and a couple of hits gave the Giants a 3–0 lead as they took the field.

Andy Locke, starting pitcher for the Giants, toed the rubber as the infield filled the air with chatter.

"Come on, Andy. Put it over. Need strikes, baby."

"No hitter, no sticker."

Andy set the first two batters down in order but surrendered a single to the Braves catcher, Tony Bonuccelli. Billy

Porter drilled a double off the left center-field fence and the Braves had runners on second and third, two outs.

"Come on Andy, bear down."

"No hitter, no hitter."

Susan Young, the Braves center fielder, smacked a hot shot to Jamie's left. Jamie scampered over and reached out, but the ball bounced off his glove and skipped into the outfield. The runners, who were off at the crack of the bat, sprinted home. The Giants lead was cut to 3–2.

Jamie stared at his glove and put an angry fist in the pocket.

"Tough chance, Jamie," Alex called over from third. "Get the next one."

The next batter, Edmundo Gonzales, lofted a pop fly in back of third. Alex back-pedaled quickly, as Jamie, running full speed, angled toward the third-base line. At the last possible moment, Jamie shouted, "I got it." Alex stopped short as Jamie made a basket catch just in fair territory for the third out.

The two buddies jogged into the dugout together.

"Glad you called me off," Alex said. "I don't think I could have gotten that one."

"No sweat," Jamie smiled. "It was about time I caught one."

FOURTEEN

The Giants and Braves battled hard the next few innings. The Giants added two runs in the top of the third when Jamie walked, Alex doubled, and Sharon Hanley knocked them both in with a clutch two-out single. But the Braves tied it up 5–5 in the bottom of the fourth when Billy Porter turned around a Mike Baker fastball and sent it soaring over the left-field fence for a three-run homer.

"Man," Jamie whistled to Alex as the home-run ball bounced on the basketball court. "That almost conked Gretzky right on the head."

Mr. McKenna greeted his team as they tumbled into the dugout after the fourth inning. "Tie game, guys. Gotta get them back. Sharon leads off. Adam on deck. Mike's in the hole. Look 'em over, we need baserunners."

The Giants could not get a single baserunner as they went down in the top of the fifth, one-two-three. The Braves also went quietly in the bottom of the inning, as Alex snagged a hot liner and Tessie ran down a couple of lazy flies in center field.

Mr. McKenna was full of encouragement as the Giants came up in the top of the sixth and final inning.

"Tyler. Tessie. Jamie. Last ups, guys. Everybody hits this inning. Let's go. Gotta make something happen."

Tyler Phelps, the Giants substitute right fielder, made something happen by slicing a single into right field. Tyler hustled to second when the right fielder bobbled the ball.

Mr. McKenna called Tessie Thomas over and whispered into her helmet as the Giants leadoff hitter nodded.

On the first pitch, Tessie squared around and plopped a perfect sacrifice bunt down the third-base line. Tyler sprinted to third as the Braves third baseman threw to first.

Runner on third, one out.

Jamie stepped to the plate. The Braves infield was drawn in to the edge of the grass, hoping to cut off the run at the plate. Jamie held up on a low fastball.

"Ball one!" The umpire called.

Jamie was looking for a pitch higher in the strike zone. *A fly ball, and the runner on third can tag up*, Jamie reminded himself.

The next pitch was about belt high. Jamie swung and connected. As Jamie ran to first base, he wondered whether he had got enough on the ball. He glanced toward the outfield to see the Braves center fielder drifting back to settle under the fly ball.

Tyler Phelps waited at third base until the ball was caught and then dashed home in front of the throw.

The Giants were ahead 6–5!

One out later, the Giants hustled out to the field desperately hoping to defend their razor-thin margin.

Jamie brought Alex, who had made the last out of the inning, his glove and hat.

"All right, Jamie!" said Alex, taking the glove and hat. "One-two-three inning coming up. Nothing gets by us this inning."

Jamie nodded, but he was not really sure. He had not fielded a ball since the first inning pop-up. One good play, one error. He was fielding .500. Same as his batting average.

The inning started poorly. Mike Baker, the Giants pitcher, walked the first batter on four shaky pitches.

"Come on, Mike," Jamie chattered nervously. "Put it over. Force at second, Sharon."

The next batter swung at the first pitch and scorched a grounder up the middle. Jamie dashed to his left to get in front of the ball. Keeping his hands back, he scooped up the grounder then flipped the ball to Sharon, who was alertly covering second base.

One out, runner on first.

The Giants infield was again filled with baseball chatter.

"Nice play, Jamie."

"Good heads-up, Sharon."

"Force at second, again."

"Get it over, Mike."

Mike Baker grooved the next pitch, and the Braves batter slapped a clean single to left.

Runners on first and second, one out.

The runners moved up to second and third as Mike tossed his next pitch in front of the plate and the ball bounced behind the catcher.

"Settle down, Mike."

"Throw strikes, baby."

Jamie and Alex had a quick conference on the left side of the infield.

"Should I play up?" Alex called from third.

"You play up to cut off the run at the plate," Jamie instructed. "I'll play back to keep the runner at second from scoring."

The next Braves batter worked the count to three balls, one strike, and then sent a line drive rocketing between shortstop and third base. Jamie took one quick step to his right and leaped. The ball wedged into the webbing of his battered mitt. Jamie snapped his hand shut before he tumbled to the infield dirt.

The runner on third, who had started for home, desperately scrambled back to third.

"Cover the bag, Alex," Jamie shouted, raising himself to his knees on the infield dirt.

Alex, still celebrating Jamie's acrobatic catch, hesitated and then darted back to third. Jamie's flip throw was a split second late.

Safe!

Alex slammed the ball into his glove. "Sorry, Jamie," Alex said. "Great catch."

Jamie signalled the other fielders. "Two down."

"No batter, no batter," Jamie called out, but did not believe it. Billy Porter stepped to the plate and stared out at the pitcher.

The Braves star slugger worked the count to two balls, one strike and then lashed a hard grounder into the hole between short and third. Jamie ranged a few quick steps to his right. Keeping his hands back, he scooped up the grounder that skidded just a few inches in front of his glove. *Yes!* he thought. *This is the way it's supposed to feel!* Jamie set his right foot and threw as hard as he could to first base.

The Giants first baseman, Adam Kinner, stretched out. The ball smacked into his mitt a blink of an eye before Billy Porter raced across the bag.

"Out!" the umpire shouted. The Giants had won 6–5!

FIFTEEN

Jamie and Alex sat with their legs stretched out and their backs leaning against the top row of a small, metal grandstand. They were keeping an eye on Brad's minor-league baseball game. But mostly the two boys were warming themselves in the sun and the memory of the day's earlier triumph.

"All right," Alex said, holding out his hand. "Undefeated. Maybe the Giants will win 'em all this year."

Jamie slapped Alex's hand and laughed. "At least we won't lose 'em all," he said.

"We can stay undefeated," Alex said. "Now that the man with the golden glove is back. You made some great plays in the last inning.

"Hey, what did Porter say to you after the game when the teams shook hands?"

"Great play," Jamie reported.

"He didn't wise off?"

Jamie shook his head. "No, he was a good sport about it. I'm telling you, Alex, he's not so bad. Give him a break."

Alex shrugged doubtfully.

The boys leaned back and watched the game. A batter fouled a pitch off, sending the ball sailing over the backstop and into the high grass of an unmowed field in back of the baseball diamond.

As if connected by the same thought, Jamie and Alex left their gloves, tumbled off the grandstand and sprinted toward the high grass.

"Bet you a soda I find the ball before you," Alex called.

"You're on," Jamie answered, dashing toward the field.

The two friends plunged in, sweeping the high grasses aside with their hands.

"Yuck!" Alex cried. "Look at this mud!"

A soft brown ooze puddled about Jamie's feet as he moved farther into the tall grass.

Jamie searched from side to side, hoping to catch sight of the ball. As Jamie peered into the grasses, he saw something. But it was not white and round, it was brown and flat and half stuck in the mud.

It was a baseball glove.

"I got it!" called Alex from another part of the field. "You owe me a soda."

Jamie leaned over and picked the glove up from the muck. It was heavy with rain-water and caked with mud. He wiped the mud off as he opened the pocket of the glove. A signature was barely visible on the wet brown leather.

José Reyes.

Alex came over, smiling and flipping the baseball in his hand.

"That soda is gonna taste great. Come on, Jamie, pay up."

Jamie said nothing. He just stared at the glove.

"What's that?" Alex asked.

"My glove," Jamie answered.

"You mean the one you lost?"

"Yeah."

"Where did you find it?"

"Right here in the mud and stuff."

Alex touched the muddy thumb of the mitt. "It doesn't look so hot," he said. "Maybe you can dry it off or something."

Jamie nodded silently. He was thinking. Jamie ran his fingers across the glove he had oiled so carefully that winter. A thin ridge of water bubbled up from the peeling leather.

"Hey, maybe the Porters did steal it," Alex said, his voice rising with excitement. "They probably never took it home. They didn't want you to have it so they just chucked it in the field."

Jamie shook his head firmly.

"I don't think so," he said. "The Porters live on the other side of the park. They wouldn't have tossed it way over here. And anyway, look at this." Jamie held up the glove for Alex to examine.

"What am I supposed to be looking at?" Alex asked, moving his head back.

"See the marks on both sides of the thumb? They look like teeth marks to me.

I'll bet a dog ran off with the glove and left it in the field."

The two boys looked at each other, their faces brightening with a sudden realization.

"Mingo!" they shouted out together.

Alex looked at the glove, then eyed Jamie and asked, "You really think Mingo took it?"

"Yeah," Jamie nodded.

"You sure that's mud on the glove?" Alex asked, grinning.

"Gross! You're disgusting, Alex," Jamie cried out with a laugh.

The two friends started walking back to the grandstand.

"What are you going to do with the glove?" Alex asked. "Maybe you could get Pete to fix it up for you."

"Nah," said Jamie, looking out to the minor-league game. "I think I'll go to Pete and have him fix it up for Brad. He's gonna need a bigger glove."

Alex stopped walking. "Are you kidding?" he said. "After everything we went through, you're gonna give away the golden glove? Don't you remember that pickup game? Man, that glove was magic."

"I remember," said Jamie, still walking toward the grandstand. "But I don't need that glove anymore."

"Why not?"

"I've got one," said Jamie, reaching up to take his glove down from the top row of the grandstand.

"That old thing?" Alex blurted out.

Jamie looked straight at Alex.

"You said a minute ago that I fielded pretty well with this 'old thing.' You said the man with the golden glove was back."

Alex was quiet for a moment. Finally, he said, "So you think you can field just as well with that one?"

Jamie nodded. "Yeah, that's exactly what I think."

"Know what I think?" Alex said, flipping the muddy baseball up in the air.

"What?"

"I think you still owe me that soda."

THE END

Gloves
The Real Story

In the early days of baseball, ballplayers did not wear baseball gloves. The players caught the ball with their bare hands. (The players needed both hands to catch the ball.)

Playing catcher wasn't easy back then. A catcher's hands got badly bruised from the constant thump of fast-flying balls. In 1869, Doug Allison, a catcher for the Cincinnati Red Stockings, asked a saddle maker to make him a pair of leather gloves to protect his sore hands. Allison was probably the first player to wear a glove in a baseball game.

It was a while before other players followed Allison's example. Players worried that people would call them "babies" and think they weren't tough enough to play without gloves. In 1875, Charles Waitt, a second-rate outfielder for the St. Louis Brown Stockings, began to wear gloves the color of his skin. He was hoping nobody would notice, but people made fun of him anyway. The opposing fans hooted at him when he walked out onto the field.

Eventually ballplayers began swallowing their pride and putting on gloves. Albert Goodwill Spalding, the great Chicago White Stockings pitcher, was the player who turned things around. In 1877 he moved from the pitcher's mound to first base and started wearing a black leather glove. Nobody made fun of Spalding. They didn't dare. He was a superstar. Instead of laughing at him, players imitated him, buying gloves of their own. Some of the players bought their gloves from Spalding's sporting goods store in Chicago. The Spalding company, still in business today, sells sports equipment—including baseball gloves—all over the world.

The gloves of the late 1800s were nothing like today's baseball gloves. Their only purpose was to protect the players' hands. No one had thought of designing a glove that actually helped players catch the ball.

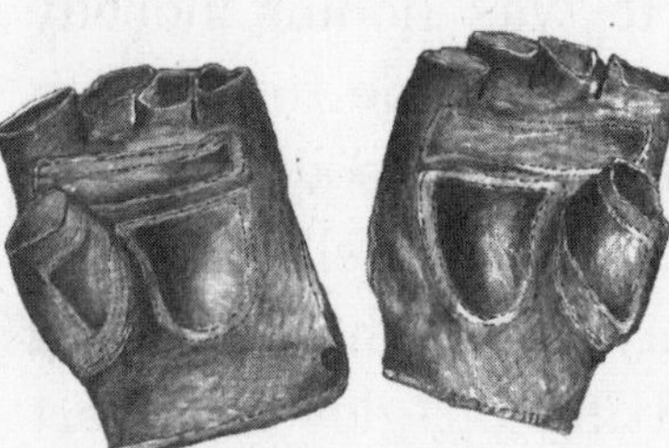

Early fingerless glove

The early gloves looked like heavy work gloves—like something a bricklayer might wear. Players often cut the fingers off the gloves because they wanted to keep their fingers free for throwing the ball. For extra padding, some players slipped strips of meat, cotton, or grass into their gloves.

In 1883, Arthur "Doc" Irwin, a shortstop for a team called the Providence Grays, broke two fingers playing ball and asked a glove maker to make him a glove with extra padding. The oversized, padded glove the glove maker created did more than protect his hands; it actually improved his fielding. Other players watched Irwin make incredible catches and decided they needed oversized padded gloves, too. Glove makers started to make more of them.

Two big breakthroughs came around 1920. A pitcher for the St. Louis Cardinals, Spittin' Bill Doak, came up with the idea of a preformed pocket that would help players hang onto the ball. Doak also came up with the idea of lacing pieces of rawhide between the thumb and the first finger of his glove. It made a web to help catch the ball. The rawhide lacing was more flexible than the wide patch of stiff leather that connected the thumb to the first finger on the early gloves.

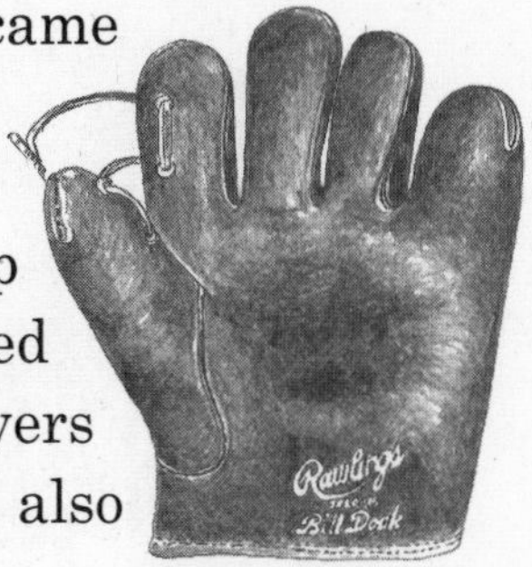

1922 Rawlings Bill Doak glove

Doak took his ideas to the Rawlings sporting goods company and Rawlings knew they were winners. The Bill Doak improvements changed the way players thought about gloves. Finally, here was a glove that was specially designed to improve fielding. Orders started coming in from all over the country.

The Bill Doak glove has become bigger and better through the years. Since the 1920s, baseball gloves have doubled in size: from six inches to twelve inches from the heel to the tip of the fingers. In present-day baseball, fewer errors are committed, fielding averages are higher, and ballplayers make catches every day that would have been unthinkable long ago.

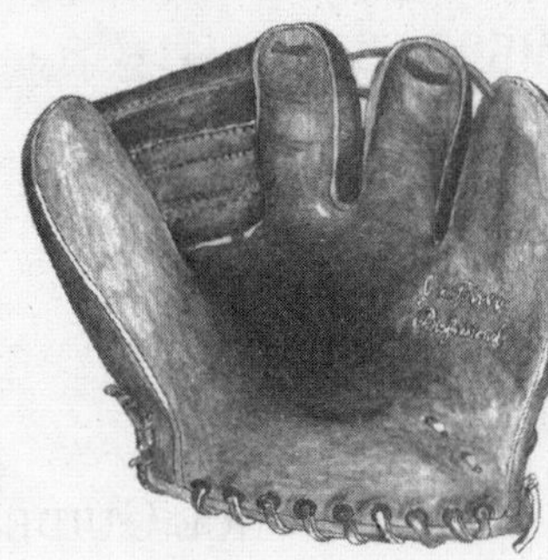

1940s Nokona three-fingered fielder's glove—two fingers fit into the little finger channel

But it has never been the glove that made players great—Hall of Famers like Pittsburgh Pirates shortstop Honus Wagner, made some extraordinary plays with some "un-extraordinary" gloves.

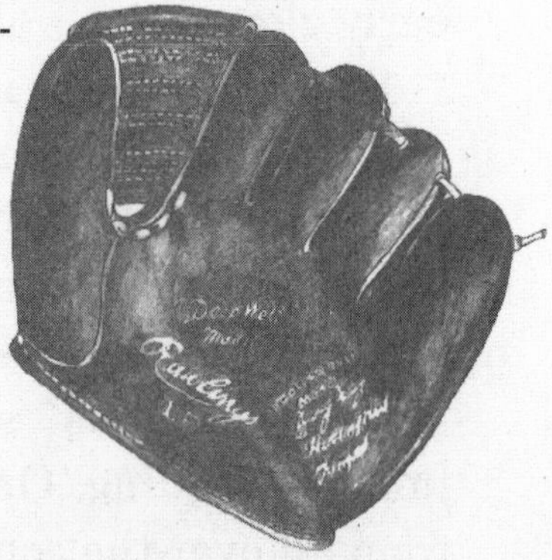

1950s Rawlings "Deep Well" fielder's glove

Pete's advice to Jamie is true. From the early days when players like Doug Allison, Charles Waitt, and Albert Spalding strapped on the first baseball gloves, "it's never been the glove that made the ballplayer. It's always been the other way around."

Guidance for glove illustrations taken from VINTAGE BASEBALL GLOVE PRICE GUIDE, Vol. 1, No. 1 © 1922 by Joe Phillips and Dave Bushing.

Acknowledgments

The author would like to thank Scot Mondore in the research department at the National Baseball Hall of Fame in Cooperstown, New York. Mr. Mondore was a terrific help in digging up interesting facts about baseball gloves.

Joe Phillips, owner of the Glove Collector in Dallas, and Geoff Phelps at the Spalding company were also very helpful.

Another valuable source of information was a May 7, 1990, *Sports Illustrated* article, “Glove Story,” written by Steve Wulf and Jim Kaplan.

About the Author

One of Fred Bowen's earliest memories is watching the 1957 World Series with his brothers and father on the family's black-and-white television in Marblehead, Massachusetts. Mr. Bowen was four years old.

When he was six years old, he was a batboy for his older brother Rich's Little League team. At age nine, he played on a team himself, spending a great deal of time keeping the bench warm. By age eleven, he was a Little League All Star.

Over a period of thirteen years, Mr. Bowen coached thirty-one different kids' sports teams in soccer, baseball, softball, and basketball.

When Mr. Bowen played Little League, he had a Spalding Glove that he loved, and lost. When he was older, he had a Wilson A2000. Now he has a Mazuna Lite-Flex, which needs relacing. He also has a SSK Dimple II that needs some oiling.

Mr. Bowen is the author of a number of sports novels for young readers. He lives in Silver Spring, Maryland with his wife Peggy Jackson. His daughter is a college student and his son is a college baseball coach.

Mr. Bowen writes a weekly sports column for kids in the *Washington Post*.

Visit his website at *www.fredbowen.com.*

Hey, sports fans!

Don't miss all the action-packed books by Fred Bowen.
Check out www.SportsStorySeries.com for more info.

Fred Bowen Sports Story series

Soccer Team Upset

PB: $5.95 / 978-1-56145-495-2 / 1-56145-495-8

Tyler is angry when his team's star player leaves to join an elite travel team. Just as Tyler expected, the Cougars' season goes straight downhill. Can he make a difference before it's too late?

Touchdown Trouble

PB: $5.95 / 978-1-56145-497-6 / 1-56145-497-4

Thanks to a major play by Sam, the Cowboys beat their arch rivals to remain undefeated. But the celebration ends when Sam and his teammates make an unexpected discovery. Is their perfect season in jeopardy?

Dugout Rivals

PB: $5.95 / 978-1-56145-515-7 / 1-56145-515-6

Last year Jake was one of his team's best players. But this season it looks like a new kid is going to take Jake's place as team leader. Can Jake settle for second-best?

Hardcourt Comeback

PB: $5.95 / 978-1-56145-516-4 / 1-56145-516-4

Brett blew a key play in an important game. Now he feels like a loser for letting his teammates down—and he keeps making mistakes. How can Brett become a "winner" again?

Want more?

All-Star Sports Story *Series*

T. J.'s Secret Pitch

PB: $5.95 / 978-1-56145-504-1 / 1-56145-504-0

T. J.'s pitches just don't pack the power they need to strike out the batters, but the story of 1940s baseball hero Rip Sewell and his legendary eephus pitch may help him find a solution.

The Golden Glove

PB: $5.95 / 978-1-56145-505-8 / 1-56145-505-9

Without his lucky glove, Jamie doesn't believe in his ability to lead his baseball team to victory. How will he learn that faith in oneself is the most important equipment for any game?

The Kid Coach

PB: $5.95 / 978-1-56145-506-5 / 1-56145-506-7

Scott and his teammates can't find an adult to coach their team, so they must find a leader among themselves.

Playoff Dreams

PB: $5.95 / 978-1-56145-507-2 / 1-56145-507-5

Brendan is one of the best players in the league, but no matter how hard he tries, he can't make his team win.

Winners Take All

PB: $5.95 / 978-1-56145-512-6 / 1-56145-512-1

Kyle makes a poor decision to cheat in a big game. Someone discovers the truth and threatens to reveal it. What can Kyle do now?

All-Star Sports Story series

Want more?

All-Star Sports Story *Series*

All-Star Sports Story series

Full Court Fever

PB: $5.95 / 978-1-56145-508-9 / 1-56145-508-3

The Falcons have the skill but not the height to win their games. Will the full-court zone press be the solution to their problem?

Off the Rim

PB: $5.95 / 978-1-56145-509-6 / 1-56145-509-1

Hoping to be more than a benchwarmer, Chris learns that defense is just as important as offense.

The Final Cut

PB: $5.95 / 978-1-56145-510-2 / 1-56145-510-5

Four friends realize that they may not all make the team and that the tryouts are a test—not only of their athletic skills, but of their friendship as well.

On the Line

PB: $5.95 / 978-1-56145-511-9 / 1-56145-511-3

Marcus is the highest scorer and the best rebounder, but he's not so great at free throws—until the school custodian helps him overcome his fear of failure.